MISSION CONTENTS

Good Vs Evil.. 6

MISSION BRIEF 1... 8

Equipment Specifications............................... 9

Battle Beneath The Waves............................. 10

Blacked Out.. 20

MISSION BRIEF 2... 22

Equipment Specifications............................... 23

Chaos In The City... 24

Stop No Face.. 34

MISSION BRIEF 3... 36

Equipment Specifications............................... 37

On Ice... 38

Time Is Running Out.. 46

MISSION BRIEF 4... 48

Equipment Specifications............................... 49

Final Battle On Island X.................................. 50

Quick On The Draw... 60

ACTION MAN XMISSIONS ANNUAL 2006

Pedigree®

Published by Pedigree Books Limited
Beech Hill House, Walnut Gardens, Exeter, Devon EX4 4DH.

E-mail books@pedigreegroup.co.uk

Published 2005
Action Man and all related characters are trademarks of Hasbro
& are used with permission.
© 2005 Hasbro. All Rights Reserved.

Licensing by:

Hasbro

Properties
Group

£6.99

GOOD

ACTION MAN

Fearless, courageous and dedicated to fighting all evils that threaten the world, Action Man is highly intelligent and can adapt to any situation. Leader of Action Team, he is extremely fit and strong and a master of all unarmed combat. A weapons expert, and highly skilled computer programmer. Action Man has a great sense of humour, especially during times of great danger!

REDWOLF

Member of Action Team. An expert tracker and hunter, he has great survival skills and knowledge of natural remedies. This eagle eyed bowman is an intuitive and spiritual master of the outdoors who can communicate with animals. A man of few words, Red Wolf has a wry sense of humour.

FLYNT

World Surf Champion at 19, Flynt is an expert of all adrenaline sports. (This includes surfing, dirt surfing, base jumping and rock climbing). Brash and loud, Flynt enjoys life to the full. He is a master of the boomerang, and one of the top computer programmers in the world.

EVIL

DR-X

Cruel, cowardly and cunning, Dr. X is a diabolical megalomaniac who wants nothing less than world domination! Extremely fit and strong, this twisted genius has great knowledge of technology, bio-chemistry and genetics. His hidden chest plate houses two high-powered rocket launcher's that can be fired in an instant! With an X-ray eye that can see through anything, Dr. X is the greatest threat to world peace today. He must be stopped!

NO FACE

A terrible car accident during a getaway has left No Face's entire body horribly scarred. An expert in robotics and nano technology, he is one of the world's top sword fighting and fencing champions, and a top motorcycle rider. No Face is almost as cruel, devious and calculating as Dr.X

TOXIC ROBOT

Dr.X has used his hideous Terror Toxin to mutate his X-Robots into even more deadly Toxic Robots! Each one is now equipped with razor-sharp swords instead of arms. Obeying Dr.X's every command, they help spread the Terror Toxin, destroying everything in their path!

MISSION BRIEF

URGENT

The hideous Dr. X has harnessed animal DNA to create a Terror Toxin to harm innocent people, transforming them into an army of deadly Toxic Troopers! With this army and his Toxic Robots, Dr. X plans to take over the world! One of his secret X-Termination bases has been sighted in the deep waters of Australia's Great Barrier Reef. Make haste to the Pacific Ocean and stop this madman's diabolical scheme before its too late!!

EQUIPMENT

ORCA SEA-JET

- Polycarbonate and magnesium composite construction.
- Lightweight and very strong. Powerful water-jet engine.
- 0-90 miles per hour in 7 seconds.
- 2x multipurpose Sidewinder missiles. Range 5km.

When flipped over the Sea-Jet changes to Orca mode, a hi-tech underwater stealth sub camouflaged as a killer whale.

AQUA CAMO

- Tight-fitting diver's suit made from lightweight titanium-threaded Kevlar armour.
- Retro-reflectum material refracts light to produce invisibility effect underwater.
- Built in air tank allows up to three hours deep sea diving.
- Wearer can dive to depths of two hundred feet.
- Aqua Camo comes equipped with a Spear Gun with explosive tipped spears.

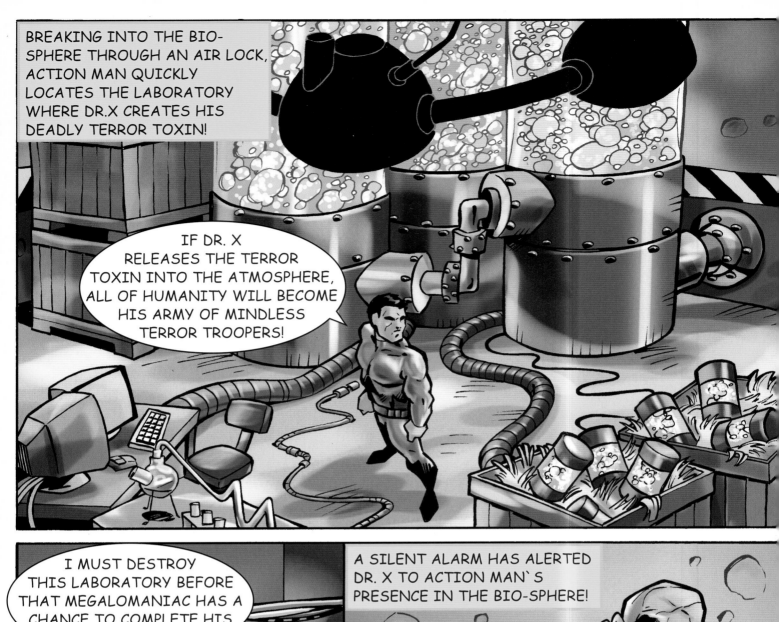

DRAGON X LUNGES UP AT ACTION MAN!

17

BLACKED OUT

ACTON MAN CALLING AGENTS! I NEED YOUR HELP! THE EVIL DR X HAS SENT A COMPUTER VIRUS TO MY LAPTOP, TURNING ALL THE IMAGES INTO SILHOUETTES! CAN YOU MATCH UP THE SILHOUETTE PAIRS, AND DISCOVER WHICH SILHOUETTE THERE IS ONLY ONE OF? WRITE YOUR ANSWERS IN THE GRID PROVIDED. ACTION MAN, OVER AND OUT!

1. ☐ MOUNTAIN RACER
2. ☐ SCUBA DIVER
3. ☐ DRAGON X
4. ☐ TIGER
5. ☐ DR X
6. ☐ ORCA SEA JET

MISSION BRIEF

RED ALERT

Dr.X and No Face have been sighted in London, England! They are planning to release the Toxic Terror Toxin inside the Houses of Parliament, turning the country's government - and the Prime Minister himself! - into members of Dr.X's mindless army of Toxic Troopers! Dr.X will then rule Great Britain! The fate of the country is in your hands. No matter what the cost, Dr.X must be stopped!!!

EQUIPMENT

TURBO BIKE

- Carbon fibre and magnesium composite with adjustable ceramic shock absorbers.
- 24 speed automatic gearbox, manual override handlebar grip.
- Two heatseeking sidewinder missiles. Range 3 km.
- GPS (Global Positioning System)
- 0-125 miles per hour in 9 seconds.
- Rocket boosters to gain maximum speed.
- Armoured helmet. Kevlar construction with anti-glare visor.

SPY PATROL

- Infra-Red hi-tech vision goggles with telescopic sight and digital zoom camera.
- Microphone earpiece with range of 100 km.
- Laptop with GPS (Global Positioning System).
- WAP phone watch with built-in explosives.
- Directional microphone to eavesdrop on criminals.

23

CHAOS IN THE CITY!

VRRROOOOMMM!
Racing through the streets of London, England, at speeds in excess of 200 miles per hour, Action Man weaved through the light, early morning Sunday traffic on his all-powerful Turbo Bike!
Just ahead of him, riding astride his deadly Power Bike, was Action Man`s target…the devious No Face!

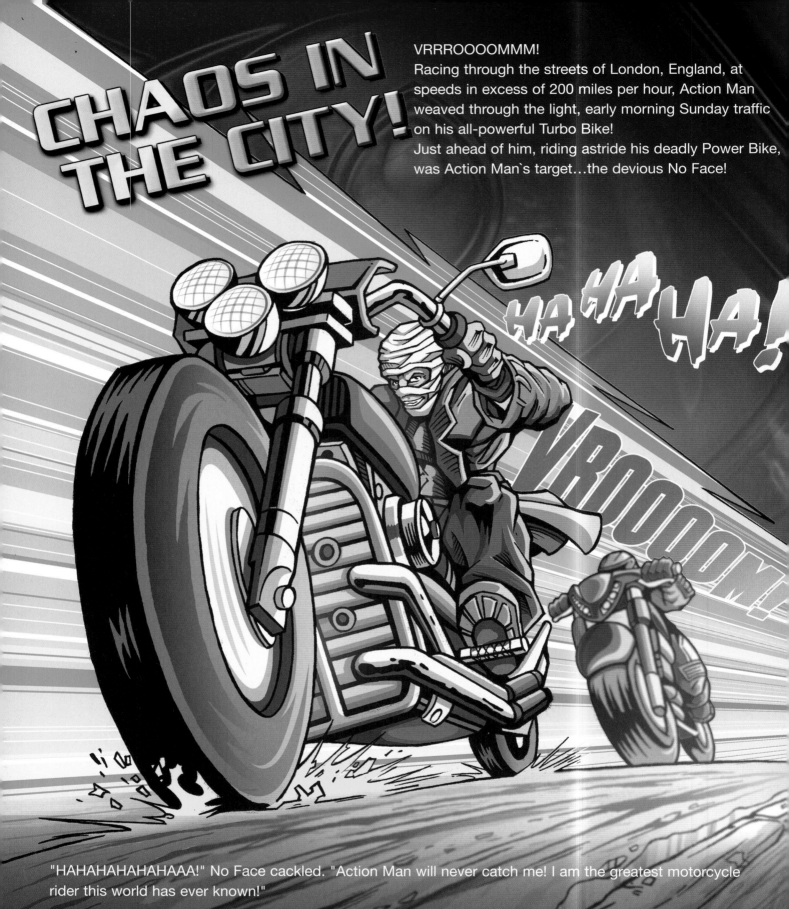

HA HA HA!

VROOOM!

"HAHAHAHAHAHAAA!" No Face cackled. "Action Man will never catch me! I am the greatest motorcycle rider this world has ever known!"

Showing off his amazing riding skills, No Face swerved into oncoming traffic! Horns blaring, terrified drivers gasped in astonishment as No Face rode up and over their vehicles - BUMPITY-BUMPITY-BUMP! - before sliding his Power Bike under the wheels of an approaching juggernaut and out the other side!
"That madman doesn`t care if he causes a serious traffic accident," growled Action Man, continuing after

His thoughts ran back to a few hours before…he had been heading towards the location of Dr. X`s secret X-Termination Base, which was stockpiled with the deadly Terror Toxin he was planning to use on the country`s government.
Action Man had been shocked to see No Face patrolling the streets of London with an army of Toxic Robots. The evil psychopath was revelling in the fact that soon he and Dr. X would rule Great Britain. No one would be safe!
But No Face had also spotted Action Man. Leaping aboard his Power Bike, he took off - and the chase was on!

Careful not to distract other drivers, Action Man revved his Turbo Bike, increasing his speed until he was almost upon his deadly foe.

"Follow me if you dare!" screamed No Face, wheeling past the historic landmark of the Tower of London, before heading across Tower Bridge.
Swerving onto the bridge, Action Man glanced across the River Thames and then grinned to himself. A large Royal Navy frigate was heading upriver towards the bridge.
"In the old days, the two bascules of Tower Bridge used to be raised fifty times a day to allow shipping to pass beneath it," he mused, keeping up speed with No Face. "Now it`s only four or five times a week. And I`ve got a funny feeling today is one of those days."
Action Man was extremely knowledgeable about all subjects - an agent had to be if he was going to survive. Action Man loved to read and to learn as much as he could about the world around him.

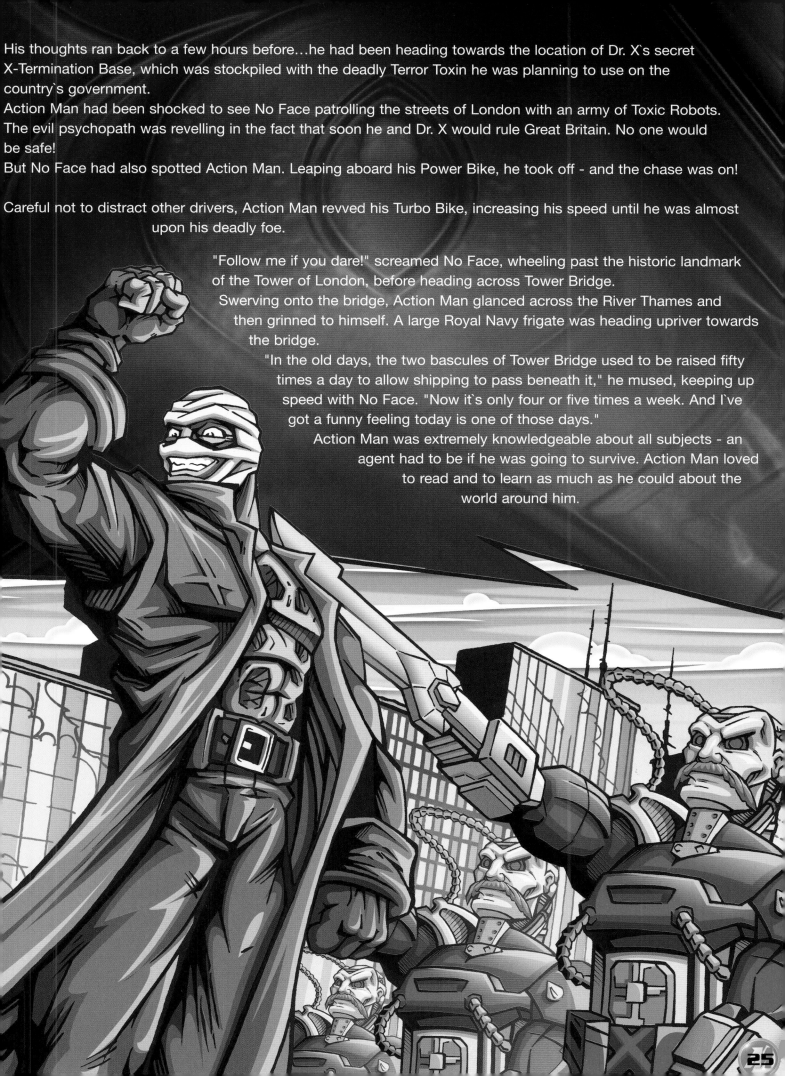

"Tower Bridge was
completed in 1894 and
named after the two
impressive towers," he
remembered, speeding past one of the
towers as he did so. "It`s 60 metres long
and 43 metres high - so if you were to fall off
the bridge, it`s a long drop to the water below!"
A plan was formulating in his mind - he now knew
how to stop No Face. But first he had to survive!
No Face suddenly spun around his Power Bike to face
him head-on.
"Now what`s he up to?" Action Man pondered…only to
discover the answer moments later when No Face fired a
miniature Sidewinder missile straight towards him! WHOOOSSSHH!
"HAHAHAHAHAAA! There`s no escape, Action Man!" screeched the
enraged No Face. "You`re going out with a bang!"
Instantly reacting, Action Man twisted the manual override
handlebar grip on his Turbo Bike, and released his own
miniature Hellfire missile with pinpoint accuracy!
WHOOOSSSHH!
The two missiles collided in mid-air! KAAA-BOOOOM!!

"Can nothing stop him?!" snarled No Face, spinning his Power Bike around and taking off again. "All Dr. X and I want to do is to rule Great Britain and then the world…what`s so wrong with that?"

Suddenly, No Face realised that apart from himself and Action Man, there were no other vehicles on Tower Bridge.
It was then that he noticed that he seemed to be riding uphill. "Eh?? How can that be?" he squealed. "The bridge was flat a moment ago!"
Action Man, in hot pursuit, chuckled to himself. "Perfect! No Face was so busy taunting me, he didn`t notice the frigate passing by underneath! That`s why the drawbridge is being pulled up! And at this speed, No Face can`t stop without falling!"
No Face revved his Power Bike to top speed. The two bascules had opened so wide he now only had one option - to take off at the top of the drawbridge and leap to safety onto the other side.

Action Man chased after him, drawing level. "Let's see who chickens out first," he shouted, grinning at a terrified No Face. Revving his engine to maximum speed, Action Man flew off the edge of the drawbridge and through the air! VRRROOOM! Landing safely on the other side, he spun around the Turbo Bike in time to see No Face follow his amazing, death-defying jump. Unfortunately, No Face's Power Bike was much too heavy!

YAAA

SPLAAASH!

"Yaaaaaahh!" No Face screamed in horror as the bike just missed reaching the other bascule. It plummeted down, down, landing with a loud SPLASSSH! in the Thames. "I've been telling No Face for ages that he could do with a bath," chuckled Action Man, watching as his helpless enemy was swept downriver.

"And now he's having one!"

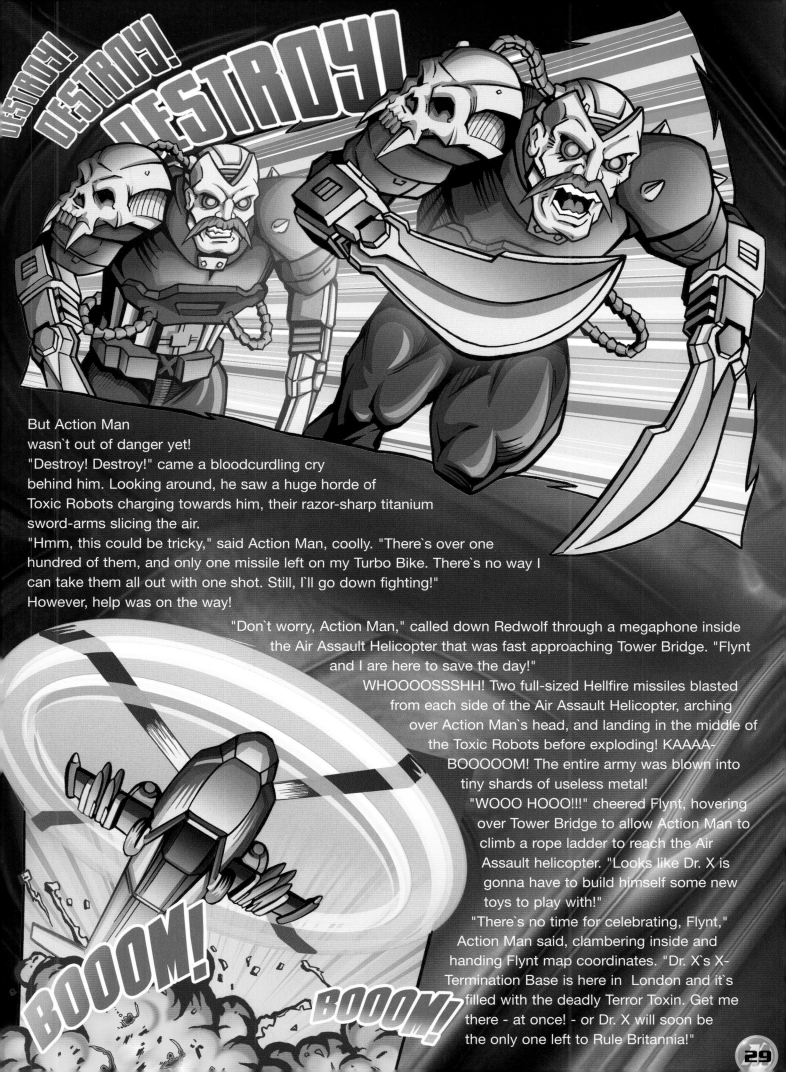

DESTROY! DESTROY! DESTROY!

But Action Man wasn't out of danger yet!
"Destroy! Destroy!" came a bloodcurdling cry behind him. Looking around, he saw a huge horde of Toxic Robots charging towards him, their razor-sharp titanium sword-arms slicing the air.
"Hmm, this could be tricky," said Action Man, coolly. "There's over one hundred of them, and only one missile left on my Turbo Bike. There's no way I can take them all out with one shot. Still, I'll go down fighting!"
However, help was on the way!

"Don't worry, Action Man," called down Redwolf through a megaphone inside the Air Assault Helicopter that was fast approaching Tower Bridge. "Flynt and I are here to save the day!"
WHOOOOSSSHH! Two full-sized Hellfire missiles blasted from each side of the Air Assault Helicopter, arching over Action Man's head, and landing in the middle of the Toxic Robots before exploding! KAAAA-BOOOOOM! The entire army was blown into tiny shards of useless metal!
"WOOO HOOO!!!" cheered Flynt, hovering over Tower Bridge to allow Action Man to climb a rope ladder to reach the Air Assault helicopter. "Looks like Dr. X is gonna have to build himself some new toys to play with!"
"There's no time for celebrating, Flynt," Action Man said, clambering inside and handing Flynt map coordinates. "Dr. X's X-Termination Base is here in London and it's filled with the deadly Terror Toxin. Get me there - at once! - or Dr. X will soon be the only one left to Rule Britannia!"

BOOOM!

BOOOM!

Night, and Action Man slipped through the darkness dressed in his Spy Patrol stealth outfit, his surveillance equipment carried in his backpack, heading towards Dr. X's X-Tower, a fifty-six storey building towering over the London skyline in the shape of a letter X!

"Perhaps I should explain to that raving madman that there is more than one letter of the alphabet," Action Man chuckled to himself.

Slipping powerful suction pads onto his hands and feet, he began climbing up the outside of the building, heading for the top floor. He knew it was here that Dr. X was storing the Terror Toxin!

A cold wind whipping at his face, Action Man took less than twenty minutes to reach his target, high above the streets of London. After using a handheld listening device to sweep the building for signs of any foes hiding in wait to attack, Action Man pulled out a powerful laser pen to cut through the strengthened glass. He quickly made a hole large enough for him to slip inside the building.

The room was pitch black. Slipping on his all purpose Vision Goggles, Action Man pressed a stud and could immediately see everything clearly in Infra-Red…including deadly disintegrating beams criss crossing the room!

"If I accidentally touch any of those beams, I`m one deep fried agent," he said, his wry humour keeping his spirits up as he began stepping over and slipping under the beams.

Cold sweat running down his face, Action Man held his breath as he carefully headed for a switch on the far wall. Time tick-tick-ticked by, but at last he reached his destination. Slapping the wall switch with the palm of his hand, a hidden door slid open beside him.

Action Man looked inside the connecting room. The lights were on, but again, it seemed completely empty.

"Dr. X should consider hiring an interior designer," snorted Action Man, stepping inside. "I've seen sewers with more flair and style!"

The door slammed shut behind him! KLAANNG! Action Man was trapped!

"Uh, oh. There might be more to this room than first meets the eye," Action Man growled. He pressed another stud on his Vision Giggles, and they changed from Infra-Red to X-Ray control! Action Man could literally see through walls!

And what he saw turned his blood cold! There were deadly iron spikes hidden inside the walls on opposite sides to him.

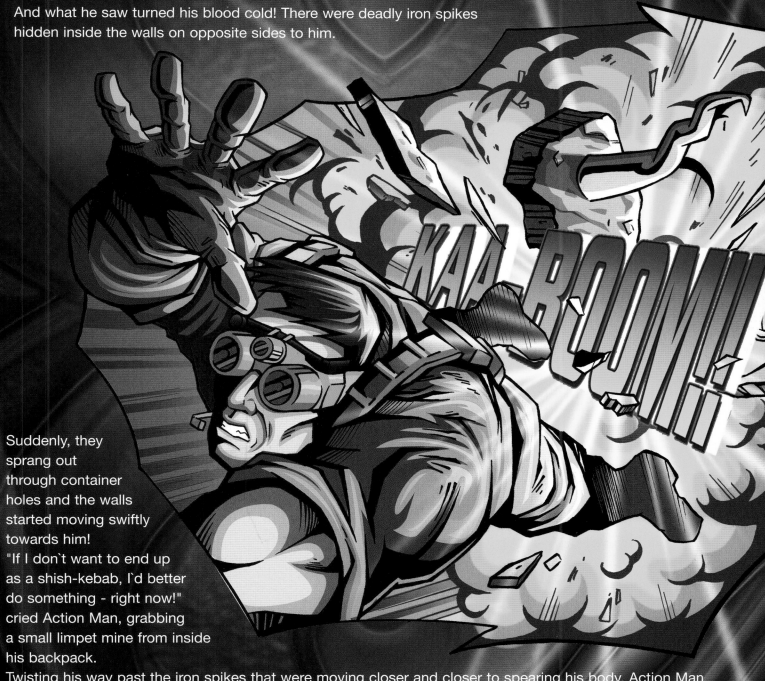

Suddenly, they sprang out through container holes and the walls started moving swiftly towards him!

"If I don`t want to end up as a shish-kebab, I`d better do something - right now!" cried Action Man, grabbing a small limpet mine from inside his backpack.

Twisting his way past the iron spikes that were moving closer and closer to spearing his body, Action Man slapped the limpet mine to one wall before diving to the other side of the room. Two seconds later, the limpet mine detonated! BOOOOOOM!!

The building rocked from the explosion, and when the dust cleared, there was a gaping hole in the wall leading to the next room…a room filled with computers, a large video screen and hundreds of vials of Dr. X`s nightmarish Terror Toxin!

Quickly attaching his laptop to the mainframe computer, Action Man used his expert computer knowledge to hack into Dr. X`s private files and began downloading all of Dr. X`s most secret information and plans for world domination.

"With this information on my laptop, Dr. X is all washed up," chuckled Action Man, disconnecting his computer when the task was done. "And now to destroy this supply of Terror Toxin!"

The video screen flickered into life. Action Man reacted to the sight of the evil Dr. X staring down at him from a hidden X-Termination Base somewhere in the Arctic Circle!

"So you think you`ve beaten me, Action Man?" he cackled. "But you will pay for your victory - with your life!"

Keeping Dr. X gloating, Action Man twisted the dial on his remote-controlled wristwatch. Parked outside the X-Tower, his Turbo Bike burst into life! VRRROOOM!

"If you`re so brave," Action Man taunted his deadly arch-enemy. "Why don`t you come here and we`ll have a final battle…face-to-face!"

Outside, The Turbo Bike released a Hellfire missile, straight at the entrance to the X-Tower! It struck with deadly force! BOOOOM!

"I don`t need to soil my hands fighting you," crowed Dr. X. "That entire building is booby-trapped with explosives!"

Revving itself up to top speed, wheels burning rubber, the Turbo Bike took off through the huge hole it had created in the X-Tower! It sped up the flight of stairs, one by one!

"And now, Action Man - goodbye!" laughed Dr. X, pressing a button on a control console. "You only have twenty seconds to live!"

The Turbo Bike burst through an interior wall, coming to a stop beside Action Man. Leaping aboard, he changed to manual override and took off, heading straight for one of the building`s huge strengthened windows. "These windows may not be broken by ordinary objects like bricks or stones," chuckled Action Man, releasing his Hellfire missile. "But I doubt even they can withstand a powerful missile attack!" KAAA-BOOOOM! Action Man was right! The window exploded outwards in a raining shower of glass, and Action Man rode straight out of the X-Tower, fifty-six stories above ground! Next moment, the entire interior of the X-Tower exploded outwards in a fiery fireball of destruction! BABA-BABA-BOOOOOM!!! Action Man had escaped - just in time!

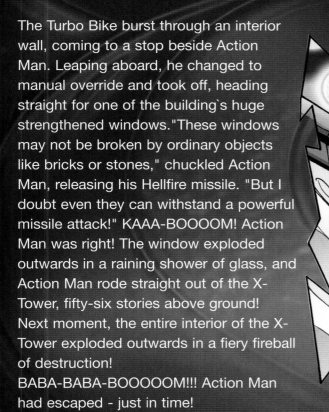

VROOOOM!

BOOM!!

KAA-BOOM!!!

BOOM!!

Plummeting down through the air, Action Man laughed! "I`m glad my Turbo Bike comes equipped with its own emergency parachute!" A large parachute attached to the Turbo Bike opened above him. "Otherwise I might have been in for a bumpy landing!"

The Turbo Bike gently descended to the streets outside the burning X-Tower.

"The Terror Toxin Dr. X was going to use to take over Great Britain has been destroyed," said a relieved Action Man, detaching the parachute before taking off again through the streets of London on his all-powerful Turbo Bike. "And I`ve downloaded enough information from his secret files to know where next to track down my deadly foe! Look out, Dr. X - here I come!"

VROOOOM!

STOP NO FACE!

The hideous No Face is tearing through the city on his Power Bike with Action Man in hot pursuit! Can you find which street entrance Action Man needs to take to catch his arch enemy?

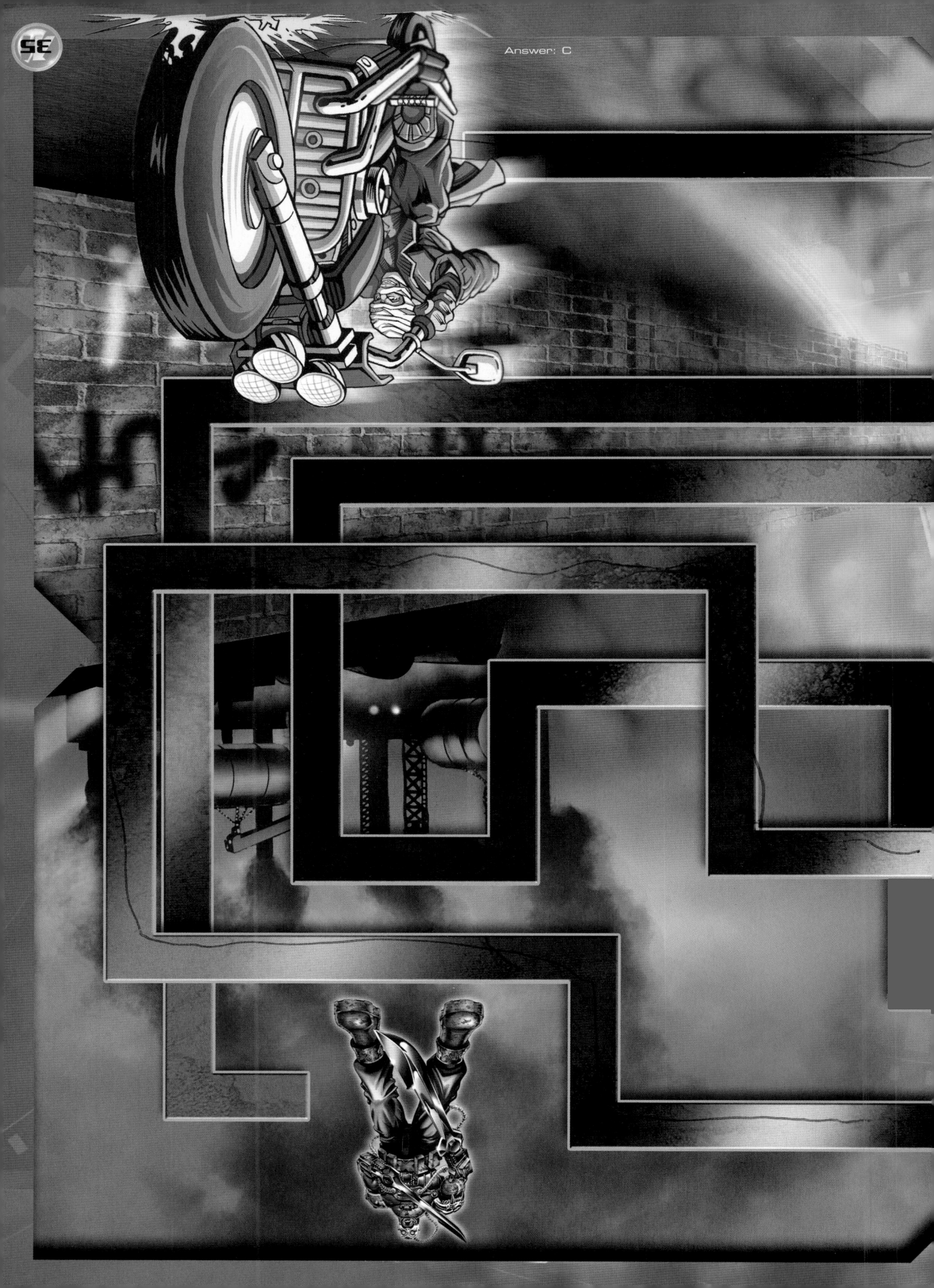

Answer: C

MISSION BRIEF

URGENT

One of Dr. X`s secret X-Termination Bases has been located deep within the Arctic Circle. The evil megalomaniac is planning to fire satellites into the upper atmosphere, releasing his deadly Terror Toxin to spread around the whole planet, turning millions of innocent people into his unbeatable Toxic Troopers. If his malevolent scheme is not halted at source, the world is doomed!

ARCTIC STORM

- Snowmobile powered by alternative fuel, designed for rapid travel over snow-covered terrain.
- Carbon fibre bonded to aluminium frame with Kevlar armour.
- Skis made from new, tough, lightweight polycarbonate material that is impact resilient.
- Can be transformed into hydrofoils to travel across water.
- Ultra-sensitive handling means the Arctic Storm can turn sharply at high speeds.
- Can reach speeds up to 160 miles per hour in clear conditions.
- GPS (Global Positioning System) connected to onboard computer.
- Massive snow cannons fire powerful destructive Plasma Bolt artillery. Range 8 km.

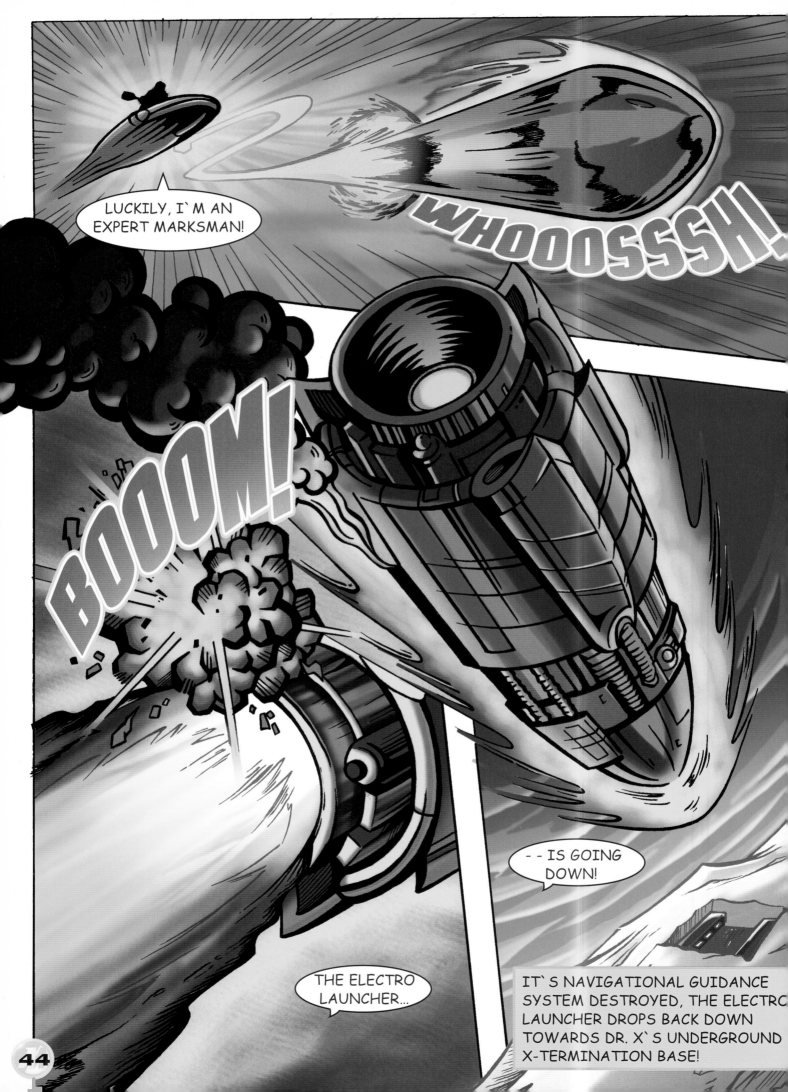

TIME IS RUNNING OUT!

Tell the times below to spell out things to do with Action Man.
Write your answer in the grid on the opposite page!

A. TEN PAST SEVEN
B. HALF PAST THREE
C. TWENTY FIVE
   PAST TEN

ACTION WATCH 3000

12 NRACER
11 ONX
1 ACTI
10 OBOT
2 SPYP
9 ONMAN
OBIKE 3
DRAG
MOUNTAI
8
4
ATROL
TOXICR
7
5
TURB
6

D. FIVE PAST NINE
E. FOUR O' CLOCK
F. TWENTY TO ELEVEN

A [Acti] [   ]

D [Spyp] [   ]

E [Oblka] [   ]

B [mountai] [   ]

F [toxic] [   ]

C [touch] [   ]

Answers: A. SPYPATROL B.TURBO BIKE C.TOXIC ROBOT D. ACTION MAN E. MOUNTAIN RACER F. DRAGON X

MISSION BRIEF

URGENT

Dr. X`s main X-Termination Base located on X-Island close to the Asian continent. Final supplies of Terror Toxin being created here. X-Island covered in impenetrable jungles and treacherous mountain terrain. Ferocious animals under the control of Dr. X patrol the island. Imperative; X-Termination Base and Terror Toxin be destroyed. Time is running out. The fate of the world rests in your hands! Good luck!

EQUIPMENT

MOUNTAIN RACER

- Carbon fibre and magnesium composite for lightness, speed and durability.
- Epoxy resin fluid-filled all-terrain tyres, which automatically change pressure to counter different surface conditions.
- Top speed 0-90 miles per hour in 4 seconds.
- Ultra-sensitive handling allows Mountain Racer to turn sharply at high speeds.
- Front-mounted razor sharp Titanium explosive discs.
- Range 1 km.

AIR ASSAULT

- Twin-engine, four-bladed multi mission attack helicopter.
- Designed to fight and survive during day and night operations and in adverse weather conditions.
- Target Acquisition Designation Sight (TADS).
- Pilot Night Vision Sensor (PNVS).
- Airspeed 200 miles per hour.
- Flight duration 7 hours.
- 16 Hellfire laser-designated missiles. Range 12000 metres.
- 1200 rounds of Plasma Bolt artillery. Range 8000 metres.
- 76 folding fin Ariel rockets. Range 5000 metres.

FINAL BATTLE ON ISLAND X

WHUP!

WHUP!

WHUP!

WHUP-WHUP-WHUP-WHUP! Screaming through the air above the Indian Ocean, Action Man flew the Air Assault helicopter with masterful skill towards his destination, X-Island, and his final showdown with the diabolical Dr. X! "The final stockpile of Dr. X`s deadly Terror Toxin is on X-Island," Action Man shouted to Flynt and Redwolf, better known as Action Team, over the thunderous noise of the Air Assault`s massive rotor blades. "We must locate and destroy it, before Dr. X can fire his Electro Launcher into Earth`s atmosphere, releasing the Terror Toxin around the planet!"

"Dr. X sure is some whacked-out wallaby," chuckled Flynt. "Doesn`t he know how hard it would be to rule the entire world??! He`d never get a decent night`s sleep, ever again!"
"My tribe has an ancient saying," spoke up the usually reserved Redwolf.

"He who wants everything is a spoilt brat!"
"So we`re going to teach Dr. X a lesson on how to behave," grinned Action Man, slicing the Air Assault through the sky, heading towards a monstrous-looking, man-made island just ahead of them. "By taking away all of his deadly toys!"

The Air Assault locked in hover mode over X-Island, Action Man, Flynt and Redwolf parachuted down towards a thick, almost impenetrable jungle.

"Dr. X will no doubt be aware of our arrival," Action Man told his companions after they had stowed their parachutes in thick brush. "So be on your guard at all times!"

Redwolf knelt, looking at light markings on the ground. He sniffed the air. "Toxic Robots have passed by here recently, heading north-by-north-west," he confirmed to Action Man and Flynt, who were in awe of his amazing tracking abilities.

"And where there`s Toxic Robots," snorted Flynt. "Dr. X won`t be far behind!"

"They will be heading for his secret X-Termination Base," said Action Man, as they followed Redwolf through the clammy, scorching heat of the jungle. "And that`s where we`ll find the last supply of Terror Toxin!"

A noise in the bushes up ahead immediately alerted Action Team to danger!

"Dr. X has populated X-Island with dozens of savage animals," whispered Action Man, the team stopping to size up the situation. "So be careful! Be very careful!"

His warning came - - too late!

With a terrifying RRROOOAAARRR!!!! a huge, ferocious tiger leapt out from the undergrowth, bowling the surprised Redwolf and Flynt off their feet!

"Uggh!" gasped Redwolf, crashing to the ground, the breath knocked out of him. "We`ve got big trouble now!"

Moving swiftly, Action Man pulled his powerful Claw Fist from his backpack, slipping it onto his wrist. "Here, kitty-kitty," he called, diving into attack. "You want to play? Then let's play!"

Wrapping his arms around the tiger, he wrenched the animal away before it could seriously injure Redwolf and Flynt. The tiger twisted free of his grasp, snarling angrily, and before Action Man could use his Claw Fist to contain the beast, pounced swiftly, knocking him to the jungle floor!

The tiger's hot, fetid breath washed over Action Man as it's razor-sharp teeth descended towards his throat!

"Hey, I'm no one's dinner!" growled Action Man, fighting back with all his raw strength. A master of all martial arts, Action Man struck with the palm of his hand a powerful kung fu Bear Thrust which sent the tiger reeling back.

Grabbing the animal around the waist, he lifted it off the ground in a Reverse Throw, and the tiger crashed back down, unharmed but slightly dazed. Aiming his Claw Fist, Action Man fired a thick nylon rope which wrapped around the tiger, trapping it! There was no escape!

"Sssssh!" said Action Man quietly, kneeling in front of the creature, soothing it with his amazing animal skills.
The tiger slowly grew calm, and before long, with Action Man scratching behind its ears, actually began to purr contentedly!
Flynt shook his head in disbelief. "Now I have really seen everything!" he chuckled, watching Action Man climb onto the tiger`s back.
"This big cat might come in handy when we meet up with Dr. X," Action Man said, directing the tiger to follow Redwolf, who once more began tracking the path towards X-Island`s secret X-Termination Base!

The trail lead out of the jungle and up a steep mountainous path.
"Ambush!" screamed Redwolf, at the appearance of a horde of deadly Toxic Robots above them.
The Toxic Robots charged down, slicing and dicing the air with their razor-sharp titanium sword-arms!
"Destroy! Destroy!" they yelled, leaping towards the outnumbered members of Action Team!

"Oh, brother!" chuckled Flynt, letting loose with his boomerang, which spun around in a wide arc, taking down eight Toxic Robots in one go! "Is that all these guys know how to say?"

Each time the boomerang struck, the Toxic Robots exploded! BOOOM! BOOOM! BOOOM!

Redwolf pulled his collapsible tungsten bow from its holster quiver and snapped it into place. "Yeah, if there`s any destroying to be done," he said, scowling, letting loose with a barrage of explosive arrows "then we`re the guys to do it!"

KAAA-BOOOOM! The explosive arrows detonated on contact, and Toxic Robots were blown to smithereens!

While Action Team kept their attackers at bay, Action Man hurriedly rode the tiger up the boulder-strewn mountain path, cutting around the Toxic Robots until he was high above, overlooking the battle.

With nothing more than his own amazing strength, he pushed a huge boulder down the mountain!

As one boulder crashed into another, and then another, Action Man watched in pleasure as the deadly avalanche of boulders fell like a heavy rain shower, smashing into the remaining Toxic Robots, destroying them all!

"If those Toxic Robots thought they had us beaten,"

he chuckled, waiting for Flynt and Redwolf to join him,

"they must have had rocks in their heads!"

Redwolf looked at Flynt, grinning. "His jokes just get worse!" he laughed.

Pulling themselves up onto a flat mountain plateau, Action Team found themselves some distance from the entrance to a huge monolithic building that stretched high into the air.

"Dr. X's final X-Termination Base," said Action Man, grimly. "Time to call in the specialised equipment!"

He twisted the dial on his remote-controlled wristwatch and - WHUP-WHUP-WHUP! - the Air Assault helicopter flew through the sky at top speed until it hovered over the plateau. It's undercarriage opened, and out parachuted Action Man's amazing Mountain Racer!

Leaping aboard, Action Man took off, speeding towards the X-Termination Base!

"Knock! Knock!" chuckled Action Man, pressing a switch to release a barrage of high-powered explosive discs. ZIIIP! ZIIIP! ZIIIP!

The discs struck the heavy titanium double doors that led into the X-Termination Base! BOOOM! BOOOM! BOOOM! The doors burst open, and Action Man drove straight through the thick, billowing smoke!

"Woo hoo!" he cheered, speeding into the building's long, deserted hallway. "Wakey, wakey, Dr. X! You have visitors!"

WHOOOOSSH!

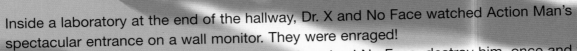

Inside a laboratory at the end of the hallway, Dr. X and No Face watched Action Man's spectacular entrance on a wall monitor. They were enraged!

"Curses!" Dr. X screamed. "Action Man has found us! No Face, destroy him, once and for all!"

"Yes, Dr. X!" cackled No Face, hurrying out of the laboratory with an army of Toxic Robots and Dragon X. "This will be - the end! - of Action Man, once and for all!"

Action Team and the tiger rushed into the X-Termination Base to join Action Man - the final battle was about to begin!

The tiger leapt upon Dragon X, both creatures fighting savagely! RRRROOOAAARRR!! HSSSSSSSS!!

"Fools!" cackled No Face, watching Flynt and Redwolf take down dozens of Toxic Robots with their boomerang and explosive arrows. "Even now, Dr. X is about to fire the Electro Launcher into the atmosphere! No one can stop him! No one! HAHAHAHAHAHAAAA!"

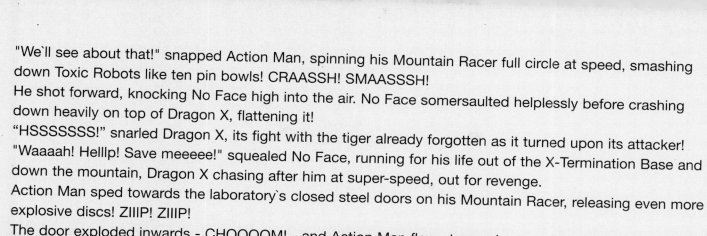

"We`ll see about that!" snapped Action Man, spinning his Mountain Racer full circle at speed, smashing down Toxic Robots like ten pin bowls! CRAASSH! SMAASSSH!

He shot forward, knocking No Face high into the air. No Face somersaulted helplessly before crashing down heavily on top of Dragon X, flattening it!

"HSSSSSSS!" snarled Dragon X, its fight with the tiger already forgotten as it turned upon its attacker!

"Waaaah! Helllp! Save meeeee!" squealed No Face, running for his life out of the X-Termination Base and down the mountain, Dragon X chasing after him at super-speed, out for revenge.

Action Man sped towards the laboratory`s closed steel doors on his Mountain Racer, releasing even more explosive discs! ZIIIP! ZIIIP!

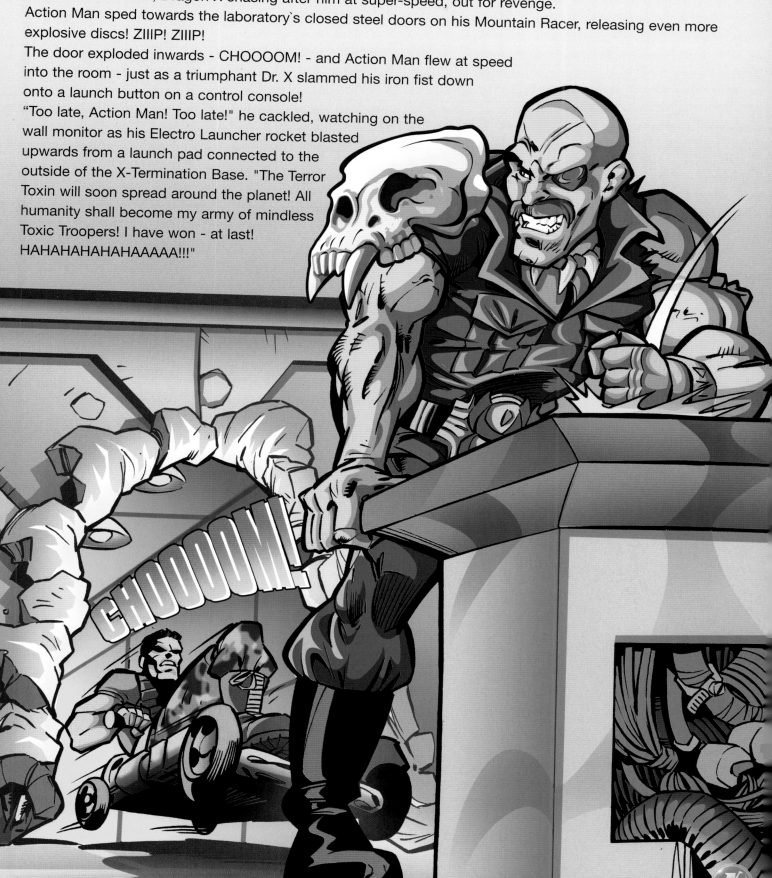

The door exploded inwards - CHOOOOM! - and Action Man flew at speed into the room - just as a triumphant Dr. X slammed his iron fist down onto a launch button on a control console!

"Too late, Action Man! Too late!" he cackled, watching on the wall monitor as his Electro Launcher rocket blasted upwards from a launch pad connected to the outside of the X-Termination Base. "The Terror Toxin will soon spread around the planet! All humanity shall become my army of mindless Toxic Troopers! I have won - at last! HAHAHAHAHAHAAAAA!!!"

Action Man chuckled. "You never learn, you madman! The world will never bow down to the likes of you!" He twisted the dial on his wristwatch. Outside, the Air Assault helicopter turned to face the X-Termination Base. 1200 rounds of Plasma Bolt artillery blasted at the Electro Launcher before it achieved any height! BUDDA-BUDDA-BUDDA-BUDDDDAAA!

The Electro launcher - EXPLODED! KAAAAAA-BOOOOOM!!! The searing heat of the explosion destroyed the final supplies of the Terror Toxin - - forever!

Next, the Air Assault let rip with 76 folding fin Ariel rockets and 16 Hellfire laser-designated missiles! WHOOOOSSSH! WHIIIISSSSHHH!

"NOOOOOOOO!!!!" screamed a terrified Dr. X, watching the rockets and missiles heading straight for the X-Termination Base. "Action Man can`t have beaten me again! He just can`t! It`s not fair!"

Not waiting for the barrage of artillery to strike, Action Man, Flynt, Redwolf and the tiger had already rushed out of the X-Termination Base, heading down the mountain.

Looking back, they watched Dr. X`s lair disappear in a massive fiery explosion that rocked the very mountain itself! KAAA-CHOOO-BOOOOOOM!!!

"Wow," gasped Redwolf, his ears ringing. When the black smoke had lifted, the X-Termination Base was nothing more than burning rubble. "Not even Dr. X could have escaped from that!"

"Don`t be too sure," said Action Man, grimly - he knew Dr. X only too well. "But if he ever does appear to threaten the world again, we`ll be here to stop him!"

Once more, the evil Dr. X had been defeated by the greatest hero of all time -

- ACTION MAN!

QUICK ON THE DRAW

Draw over the image of the evil Dr. X on the opposite page and then colour it in using this page to guide you.